Mom's Christmas Carol

Jennifer Shaw Wolf

Book Cover by Purpose on Paper

Editing by Cady Wolf

1st edition 2023

For my imperfectly perfect mom,
for teaching me what and who are most important and for the priceless
gift that is her unwavering faith.

1

Unto Us

Melody knelt down in front of her daughter Isabelle. Her arms hung down and the shimmery white fabric of her angel costume ballooned over her hands. "Remember Izzie, the line is 'Unto us a child is born,' not, 'for us a child is born,' okay? You don't want to get that one wrong. It's in the Bible so it's important." Izzie's big blue eyes reflected the stage lights and her dark curls bobbed as she nodded.

"Go change. You don't want to ruin your costume before the play tomorrow."

Izzie nodded again and ran backstage, white satin flowing behind her.

"Stop!" Melody said as two shepherds ran past her. "These are not weapons." She took the crooks the boys had been using as swords. "Make sure these and your costumes are hung up on the hook with your names," She gave them their crooks and a stern shake of her head. "We can't break or lose anything before the pageant tomorrow. Everything has to be perfect."

"Everything is already perfect." Kara laid an armload of fresh-ly-pressed angel costumes across the table. Her hazel eyes shone with admiration as she smoothed the folds of a gold headpiece from one of the wise-men's costumes before she hung it up.

"It's not bad." Melody tried to sound modest, but a sense of ac-complishment bubbled up in her chest.

"Not bad?" Kara spread her arms wide to encompass the scene before all of them. Blue and purple stage lights illuminated a silhouette of Bethlehem and the hills beyond. In front were cutouts of sheep, camels, and shop fronts. "Are you seeing what you've done here–the lights, the sets, the decorations, the costumes? How long did it take you to sew the wise men's costumes? Seriously, the whole thing is just amazing."

Melody considered the hours and money she'd spent on every part of the pageant, just hand-sewing gold braids to the wise men's robes had taken hours. As she looked at her creation, she decided the time and money she'd spent had been worth it.

Amy's tall high-heeled boots clicked across the wood floor as she joined them behind the stage. "Kara's right. This is going to go down as the best Nativity pageant ever. Not to mention the dinner, the music, and just everything."

Kara finished hanging up the costumes and tugged a red cardigan embellished with sequin-studded reindeer over her shoulders. "How do you do it? I can barely keep my kids and house together. Never mind anything extra."

"Especially wrangling three-year-old twin boys while Michael is traveling," Amy readjusted the sloppily hung shepherd's robe so it was secure on its assigned hooks. "I can't even imagine."

"I couldn't have done it without both of you." Melody stretched her arms and pulled them both into a generous hug. "It's been a team effort."

"Speaking of team," Amy glanced at her watch. "I need to get going if I'm going to pick Harrison up from basketball practice on time."

"And I'd better relieve my babysitter, Kara added.

Evelyn stepped into their circle. She was twisting a leftover piece of ribbon from her wreath-making project between her fingers. "I know it's late notice and we all need to head home, but I was just wondering...um I think it would be nice if we included...if we invited, some of the other members of our community." She took a nervous breath. "The homeless shelter is just down the street. I'm sure they would appreciate a little Christmas spirit, and I know we'll have plenty of food. I just thought..."

"Absolutely not!" Amy broke in. She brushed errant pine needles off her jeans as if she were trying to brush off any discomfort. "I mean, we could donate what's left over to them, but exposing our kids to those kinds of people? I'm just not comfortable with it."

"Never mind the smell," Kara said.

Melody put her hand on Evelyn's shoulder. "It's a good idea. Maybe for next year, when everything isn't already set. We could do a separate program and serve a soup lunch or something like that. I'll keep it in mind, that is, if they ask me to help again next year."

"Of course they'll ask you back. No one could do it better," Kara gushed.

"Right. Next year." Evelyn tucked her grey streaked brown hair behind her ear and nodded as she moved to collect her children.

"See you ladies tomorrow about 1:00." Melody waved to Kara and Amy.

For a second something tugged at Melody's conscience. She watched Evelyn tugging an oversized coat on her toddler. There were dark circles rimming her eyes and her shirt was wrinkled. She seemed tired and worried, but who wasn't during the holidays? Melody gave Evelyn a small, sympathetic smile. She wondered if she should ask her how she was doing. They used to be close, their daughters were the same age and they had spent a lot of time helping each other out, swapping playdates and babysitting. Melody had been so busy with the pageant and the holidays that they hadn't talked much in the last couple of months. *After the holidays are over,* Melody promised herself as she watched Evelyn walk out the door.

While she waited for Izzie to come out of the dressing room, Melody took a moment to look at what she'd accomplished—the beautifully painted sets, the custom-made costumes hung in perfect rows off-stage, the red and green tables centered with holly and pine wreaths around gold candles. She sighed. The last few weeks had been exhausting, but she knew the other ladies were right, this would be the best Christmas pageant the church had ever seen.

2

Christmas Chaos

"Daddy's coming home! Daddy's coming home! Izzie sang as they piled out of the car in the driveway.

"Yes he is." Melody pictured her husband walking into an idyllic holiday home. The eaves were draped in strands of twinkle lights, homemade wreaths hung on every door. The house was clean and inviting. He'd come home to the smell of pine and his favorite beef stew that had been simmering in the crockpot all day. They'd sit on the couch and read Christmas stories and then tuck the kids into bed early so they could have some much-needed couple time in front of a roaring fire.

The first sign that things weren't exactly as they should be was the whiff of piney, cinnamony, but un-stew scented air that greeted them when they walked through the door. "Oh no!" Melody ran to the cold crock pot.

"What's wrong Mommy?" Devin followed her into the kitchen.

"The crock pot is broken." Melody slapped the side of the crock-pot, as if that would make it heat up and magically cook the stew.

"Maybe you forgot to turn it on," Izzie peered over the counter.

"I couldn't have..." Melody trailed off as she remembered that right after she'd added the ingredients to the stew, Dallin had needed help with his shoes. She didn't remember pushing the start button.

"We could get McDonalds," Izzie suggested.

"Donalds! Donalds!" The twins began to chorus.

"Or pizza," Izzie added helpfully.

"No. Daddy has been eating out all week. I wanted him to come home to a home cooked meal." Melody headed for the fridge, a back-up plan already forming in her mind as she gathered up onions and cabbage. "Izzie, keep an eye on your brothers. I need to make dinner before Daddy gets home."

Melody pulled the extra stew meat from the fridge and chopped it into smaller pieces, praying that it wouldn't be too tough for a stir fry. She tossed it into the pan with chopped onions. The pan sizzled and the inviting smell of onions and cooking meat filled the room.

Melody's phone rang. She cradled it between her neck and chin while she chopped the cabbage. "Hello."

"Melody?" An unfamiliar voice croaked from the other end.

"Yes?"

"It's me, Jenna. I know I promised I'd do the cookies for the pageant tomorrow, but we've all come down with the flu and—"

"Ah!" Melody exclaimed as the knife slipped, catching the edge of her finger.

"I'm sorry for the late notice I can—" Jenna said.

"Sorry, not you, I just...I just." Melody ran her finger under the tap, feeling woozy as red streamed down the drain. She looked away and turned off the water. "I'm so sorry to hear that. We'll really miss Ben as a shepherd, but we can make do without him."

"Oh, I'm not worried about Ben. It's the cookies."

Melody wrapped a paper towel around her hand and pressed against the pain and the blood that continued to flow. "Cookies?"

"I won't be able to bring the cookies," Jenna repeated.

Her words sunk in. "You can't bring the cookies?" Melody was counting on Jenna's exquisite decorating skill to bring the wow factor to the desserts that would finish the party.

"No. Everyone is sick. I started the cookies yesterday, but it's such a nasty bug. I'd hate to get anyone else sick."

"Of course," Melody worked to keep the panic out of her voice. She took a breath and switched to compassionate mode. "Is there anything I can do to help? Dinner or—"

"Devin no!" Izzie's cry was followed by the sound of breaking glass. Melody rushed into the next room, her finger wrapped in a now blood-soaked paper towel, the phone still cradled beneath her chin.

"Actually that would be—"

"Hold on a minute." Melody worked to keep her voice calm as she assessed the damage. Devin was crying in the middle of the floor. At his feet was the cow from her Nativity set—the set her mother had hand-painted when Melody was a teenager. Its leg was lying next to a sad-looking headless donkey.

Melody sank to her knees. "What happened?"

"He was making them fight." Izzie's eyes swam with tears. "I tried to get them away from him, but he dropped them."

"Izzie, I asked you to watch your brothers!" Melody yelled. She dropped the phone as she used her good hand to scoop up the broken animal parts.

"I'm sorry Mommy." Izzie knelt down beside her and reached for the broken pieces.

"No! Don't! Take your brother away. I don't want you to get cut."

"Can you fix it?" Izzie's voice trembled.

"I don't know," Melody answered sharply.

"Melody, is everything okay?" The voice from the phone startled her. She picked it up, and realized that Jenna was still there.

"Fine." She forced a laugh. "Devin just dropped something."

"If the cookies are a problem I could have Kevin pick some up at the grocery store on his way home. He's the only one who's not sick."

Melody strained to keep her voice pleasant. "Oh no, no problem. And I'm bringing you dinner on Saturday night. No arguing."

"You're an angel, thank you," Jenna said.

"No problem." Melody said and hung up the phone. She looked mournfully down at the pieces of the broken Nativity. Each piece had been hand-painted by her mom. There was no way to fix them without making them look shabby. Water running somewhere above her head caught her attention. She stood up fast. "Izzie, where is Dallin?"

"I don't know," Izzie admitted.

Melody piled the broken pieces in the corner of the Nativity and ran upstairs to the bathroom. Water cascaded down both sides of the toilet. Bits of toilet paper floated alongside a plastic Noah's Ark and an assortment of animals caught in the ensuing flood. A guilty looking Dallin stood in the middle of the room, a pair of plastic lions in his hand.

"Dallin! What did you do?" Melody asked.

"Wouldn't go down!" He yelled, pointing at the mess of toys.

"What wouldn't go down?" Melody looked frantically from his stunned expression to the disaster in front of her. Dallin was too upset to speak. He reached his arms to her for comfort, but she pushed him out of the way as she grabbed the toilet plunger. He fell in the quickly rising flood, dropped the lions, and started wailing. Melody peered into the depths of the toilet bowl. The cause of the destruction, Noah himself, was wedged in the bottom. Melody rolled up her sleeves and reached in, jerking the prophet out like a cork. The water continued to rise.

"Who else is in there?" Melody yelled.

"Mommy something's burning!" Izzie yelled from downstairs.

"The stir fry!" For a heartbeat Melody was torn between rescuing the burning dinner and quelling the flood. Finally she gathered her senses, reached behind the toilet and turned off the water. She hoisted a soggy Dallin off the floor and ran back downstairs to the smoke-filled kitchen just as the fire alarm started to shriek. Devin and Dallin wailed along with the cacophony from the alarm. Izzie covered her ears and tears ran down her cheeks too.

Melody set Dallin down on the kitchen floor, grabbed the frying pan and charred meat off the burner and headed for the doorway. She threw open the door and flung the burnt meat and onions into the smiling face of her husband.

"Melody, what the—?" He stepped back, sheltering behind a bouquet of pine boughs and white roses as he dodged the ruined dinner bits.

Melody opened her mouth to explain. Instead she started to cry.

3

Present (Im)perfect

"It's okay, honey." He reached to pull her into his arms.

She resisted his embrace. "No it's not okay. Everything is supposed to be perfect and just look." She sweeps her arms to encompass the crying children, the smoke-filled kitchen, the broken animals from the Nativity and the flooded bathroom at the top of the stairs.

Michael stepped inside, set the flowers on the counter, grabbed a broom and knocked the wailing fire alarm to the floor. The silence after it fell was deafening. He surveyed the carnage for a long quiet moment. He turned to face his little family and proclaimed, "We all need a break. Let's get this mess cleaned up and then we'll go out for pizza. It's early enough that we might even be able to catch a movie afterwards. What was that new Christmas cartoon called again?"

"Santa and the Snow Bears!" Izzie yelled, jumping up and down with delight. The boys joined her and soon the kitchen was full of noise again.

"I can't," Melody said.

The joyful din ceased in the face of her solemn pronouncement. "I have to make cookies for the pageant tomorrow. Jenna's whole family is sick and she can't do it."

"We can just buy some cookies," Michael said.

Melody folded her arms across her chest. "I can't serve store-bought cookies after the pageant."

Michael's dark eyebrows tented in confusion. "Why not?"

Melody looked at him as if he didn't understand the basic nuances of a church Christmas party. "Maybe if I'd ordered them ahead of time from a bakery, but the only cookies available now are cheap grocery store cookies–the cheap shaped kind with sugar sprinkles."

"Sugary shaped grocery store cookies are my favorite," Michael ran his fingers through his dark hair. Obviously he still didn't understand.

"Cookies!" Dallin yelled.

"We could stay home and help you make cookies instead of going to the movies," Izzie suggested softly.

Melody shook her head. "No. They won't be good enough. Everyone's expecting Jenna's fancy cookies, not the ones we make just for fun."

Izzie's face fell.

Michael surveyed the mess around him. "O-kay what can I do? Cook dinner? Clean up the bathroom?"

"Just go." Melody looked at her family. They all blinked back at her in silent fear. She gestured to the door. "Just get them out of here."

"But Mommy," Izzie's eyes were brimming over. "I can help you clean up the mess. I'm sorry about Grandma's cow," her lip quivered, "and her donkey," her voice shook, "and the flood."

"No, just, just go, all of you!" Melody yelled. Her pent-up frustration over the burned dinner, the broken Nativity, the flooded bathroom, and the ruin of her perfect evening, poured out in anger toward her family.

"Okay. C'mon kids." Michael quietly helped Dallin change into dry clothes while Izzy found everyone's shoes. They put on their coats and headed for the door.

At the last minute Dallin ran back, and wrapped his arms around her leg. He looked up at her with big sad eyes. "Come Mommy!"

Melody peeled his little fingers from her pant leg and shook her head. "Mommy has too much to do to go play now."

4

Chains

Melody got to work as soon as they shut the door. She tried to forget hurt looks from her family that lingered long after the car had pulled away. They didn't understand that everything she was doing was for them.

She shook off her own exhaustion and bandaged her finger. Then she cleaned up the mess in the kitchen, rescued Noah's wife from the depths of the toilet, and mopped the floor. She swept the entire Nativity set into a box and put it in the back of the closet. She didn't have time to deal with it now.

Once the house was in order she started on a giant batch of sugar cookies. A pang of guilt hit her as she measured out the sugar. She thought of how Izzie had sprinkled the white sugar over the butter last year, pretending she was sprinkling snow over little yellow houses. Decorating cookies was Izzie's favorite thing to do at Christmas, but Melody didn't have time for Izzie's help now. She washed her hands and put the cookie dough in the fridge to chill.

There were still a million things to do, but she was so tired. She sat down on the couch. A few minutes with her eyes closed and then she'd be back to work. The cookie dough needed to chill anyway. She made a mental list of everything she had to do to be ready for the pageant tomorrow. Exhaustion took over and she drifted off to sleep.

Something rattled across the floorboards on the back porch. She blinked awake, looking toward the sound. A familiar face reflected in the glass of the French doors. Melody bolted upright and looked again. The image was gone. She rubbed her eyes. She had to be dreaming or having some kind of stress-induced hallucination. The person she thought she'd seen couldn't really be there.

The rattling came again. She stood up and crept closer to the door. "M-Mom?"

"Hello darling."

Melody spun around as the pale apparition glided to the couch behind her, then plunked herself down with a resounding clank. She was wearing a fluffy pink robe, a pair of feathered slippers, and a long metal chain that coiled from her neck to her ankles.

"Mom, it can't be...I...you...you're..."

"The word you're searching for is dead." The specter adjusted her robe. "I prefer 'moved on', 'relocated to a new dimension', or 'gone to a better place'." The ghost of her mother reclined back and crossed her bare legs at the ankles, the chains clanking against each other like an overdone haunted house sound effect.

"But why are you here? And what are you wearing?" Melody asked.

Her mother laughed and smoothed her hands down the front of her robe. "Do you like it? It's the latest rage among the fashionably deceased. Most prefer a solemn white satin, but for me—"

"No, I mean the chains. Why are you in chains, Mom?"

Her mother's bright smile faded. "I wear the chains I forged in life—chains of pain, chains of sorrow, but mostly chains of regret."

"Regret? But you were a good person, a good mom," Melody insisted. "You did everything you could to make the best life for me and Erin and you were always helping other people."

The specter reached down and unwound one of her chains from the leg of the coffee table. "Everyone who walks this life has regrets. Maybe mothers most of all." For a moment the spirit's eyes seemed to grow misty. "But it's not too late for you, darling. Tonight you'll be visited by spirits who can help you overcome the chains you're forging, even now. But beware. If you don't listen to them, your chains will be far heavier than mine."

"But Mom. I don't have time to visit with spirits tonight. I have cookies to bake and I still need to—"

Her mother leaned forward and patted Melody's hand. "Hush darling. You have all the time you need. In fact, in the realm of spirits, sometimes time can even go backwards."

Melody drew back from her mother's ghostly touch. "What's that supposed to mean?"

"Be ready, the first spirit will come with the chime of eight o'clock." Her mother's voice faded into the darkened room.

5

Christmas Past

"Mom?" Melody blinked, but the spirit was gone. She stood and shook off the vision. "I really need to get more sleep." She said to the empty room. She took a breath as she stood and tried to shake off the remnants of the dream or vision or hallucination–whatever it was. She headed into the kitchen. "Right now I need to—"

The grandfather clock in the foyer chimed eight times.

"How did it get so late?" She reached to open the fridge door, but the handle looked all wrong. In fact, the fridge itself was all wrong. Instead of the new, stainless-steel fridge she'd had since they moved into their house two years ago, she stood in front of an old white fridge with a crack in the handle that was covered in grimy fingerprints. She drew her hand back and stared at the picture stuck to the front with a pineapple magnet. It was a drawing of a flower she'd made in eighth grade. Next to it, stuck with a strawberry magnet was a picture of her and her sister when they were very little. She turned around to find herself in the kitchen of the tiny apartment where she grew up.

"You promised we could make cookies," A child's voice called from behind her.

Melody turned to answer Izzie, but instead saw her little sister. "Erin?"

"Well there aren't enough eggs in the fridge, or butter, and only a little flour in the jar, so that's not happening today. We're too poor for cookies." A defiant teenaged version of herself stood in the middle of the kitchen floor. She had her hand on her hip and was staring down at a messy-haired, seven-year-old version of Erin.

"Don't tell her that," Adult Melody said, trying to step in front of her teenage self. Teenage Melody ignored her. "Even if we had those things, we couldn't make cookies, we have to use them to make real food."

Even as she tried to convince herself that none of this was real, she felt how much those words must have stung Erin. "Erin, I'm sor—"

"They can't see you or hear you." Melody spun around. Amidst a pile of dirty dishes sat a little girl in a ruffled red and green plaid dress. She had a large red bow atop her glowing white hair.

"Who are you?" Melody asked.

"I am the ghost of Christmas Past." The spirit jumped off the counter and gave a little curtsy. "I'm a representation of your youth and innocence and all the gifts that you've been given in the past."

"She doesn't look so innocent to me." Melody pointed to the defiant sneer on her teenage self. "And this is a home where there weren't many gifts to go around."

Little Erin stomped her foot. "I wanted to make cookies so Mommy would have something for Christmas."

Melody opened the fridge. "See, empty. It doesn't matter what you want." The shelves were bare except for a bowl of leftovers, a stick of butter, one egg, and half a gallon of milk.

Footsteps outside the door made both girls turn. The door opened. A younger, bone-weary yet still cheerful, version of Melody's mother stepped across the threshold. She was wearing an old coat over her motel maid's uniform. She held a big box wrapped in plaid wrapping paper and tied with a big red bow.

"Mommy!" Erin cried. "I wanted to make you cookies, but Melody wouldn't let me."

"There's nothing to make cookies with," Melody said, leaning against the counter. "I'm starving. Did you get groceries?"

Her Mom's brown eyes glowed with anticipation. "I got something better." She set the box on the table. "Come open your present, girls." The two girls crowded around the box. Carefully they opened the lid and looked inside. It was full of smaller wrapped packages.

Erin took out the first one and carefully unwrapped an angel with eyes the same blue as Izzie's. "Oh!" she breathed.

Teenage Melody opened the next one, a tall wise man with a long gold braid running the length of his purple robe. She looked at her mom accusingly, "How did you pay for these? We don't have any extra money."

The hurt look in her mother's eyes pricked at Melody's heart. She knew how hard her mom had worked during those years just to make sure they all had enough, even if it was never enough.

"I did some cleaning for the woman who owns the ceramics shop. She let me choose one piece per month to paint and fire."

Melody counted the pieces: Mary, Joseph, and Baby Jesus, three wise men, two shepherds, an angel, a cow and a donkey. She turned to the little spirit. "It took her almost the whole year of extra cleaning and painting to complete the entire set. Why didn't she spend that time at home with us, or at a job where they would pay her in something besides ceramics?"

"Because your mother knew the true value of this gift." The spirit nodded back at the little family, now gathered around the table. Erin and teenage Melody were reverently arranging the figures in the center of the table while their mother read the Christmas story from the Bible.

"There was no tree, no ornaments, no other presents, and I think we had boxed mac and cheese for Christmas Eve dinner that year." Melody watched her teenage self help her little sister line up the wise men and shepherd around the Christ-Child. "But we had each other. And we had our faith."

"Spirit I—"

But the little girl was gone. In fact, the whole apartment was gone. Melody stood on a snowy sidewalk. In front of her, a young woman stared at a department store window display. After a moment she recognized another younger version of herself. As she stood behind her, Melody could only see the young woman's reflection in the window, not her own. The ghost of Christmas appeared next to her.

"I remember this now. We'd been married for just less than a year. We had nothing—no money, we lived in a tiny basement apartment. I'd graduated just a few weeks before, but I couldn't find a decent job. Michael was in his second semester of law school." She sighed. "Look at me, staring at all the things we couldn't afford back then."

"Are you sure that's what you're looking at?" The spirit pointed back to Young Melody.

The young woman turned from one side to the other, pulling her coat tight against her stomach. She appeared worried, but at the same time there was a glow of excitement in her eyes.

"Oh," Melody covered her mouth with her hand. "I forgot."

The young woman was so busy examining her reflection that she didn't notice the bus that pulled in or the young man who got off and then walked up behind her until his face appeared next to her in the store window.

He put his arms around her waist. "Excuse me Miss. I'm looking for a crazy woman."

Younger Melody turned, fighting back a smile. "There are a lot of crazy people out there. You're going to have to be more specific. Could you describe her?"

"Well, she's beautiful; dark hair, blue eyes. Not too tall, not too short. Perfect really."

"Oh yeah? What makes her crazy then?" Younger Melody said.

"She walked four blocks in the freezing cold and snow on Christmas Eve, by herself, to wait for the bus."

"Now that would be crazy," Young Melody replied.

"Oh, that's not the crazy part." He stood back shaking his head, like he couldn't believe what he was about to tell her. "The crazy part is who she walked all that way to meet."

"Interesting. Who was that?" Younger Melody asked.

"A beaten-down, nearly penniless, law student." He leaned closer and whispered. "And the worst part is, he's not even that good-looking."

"Hmmm, she does sound crazy." Younger Melody nodded. "But it's probably a good thing she isn't here because if she saw you, I'm sure she'd give up on her penniless, not very good-looking student, and fall for you instead."

"Like I said. She's crazy." He leaned over and kissed her. They pulled apart, his hands still on her shoulders. "So besides the fact that you're crazy, why in the world are you standing out here in the snow?"

"Because I couldn't wait until you got home to give you your Christmas present." She reached into her pocket.

Melody took a breath.

Michael's face fell in an expression of sad regret. "I thought we decided, no gifts."

"This is kind of a surprise." She drew out a little box with a bow on it. "And it's really for both of us."

Michael untied the bow and looked inside. He stood stunned for a few minutes. Then he carefully pulled out a positive pregnancy test. "Is this for real?"

Young Melody nodded silently. Her eyes filled with tears.

"He must have been terrified." Melody breathed. "He had years of school left. We had no money. I was stuck doing alterations at the laundromat. He was already working two jobs and somehow managing school."

"And yet..." The spirit said.

"This is awesome!" Michael leaned over and picked her up, spinning her around. "This is the best Christmas present we could ever have!"

Tears collected in Young Melody's eyelashes. "Are you sure? I mean, it isn't the best time."

He put his hands on either side of her face, brushing the tears away with his thumbs. "How could you think I would be anything but happy about this?"

"I don't know. It's just...just a lot."

"It's huge," he admitted, pulling her closer. "And I didn't get you anything."

"I think this one is big enough for both of us." Young Melody leaned her forehead against his. "Merry Christmas, Michael. I love you."

"Love you forever, Mel."

The swirling snow enveloped the pair as they kissed.

6

Christmas Present

Melody woke up with a start. She was back on the couch. She sat up. "Michael?" She called, but the house was empty. She picked up her phone. It was two minutes to nine. "It's so late. Where are they?"

She sent a text to her husband:

> Where are you??? The kids need to be in bed. We have
> a busy day tomorrow!

"Oh! The cookies!" She hurried into the kitchen and pulled the cookie dough out of the fridge.

The grandfather clock chimed nine times.

She turned to set the bowl of cookie dough down on the counter, but the counter was gone. She stood in the parking lot of a grocery store. Snow swirled around her bare feet. Even though she couldn't feel the cold, she walked in, still carrying the bowl of cookie dough. A bell-ringing Santa at the door followed her inside.

She wandered the aisles, not sure why she was there. Familiar voices led her to the baking aisle. Dallin was asleep in the bottom of a grocery cart. Devin chewed sleepily on a half-eaten sugared grocery store cookie. Michael and Izzie were looking at decorating supplies.

Melody walked up to them. "Michael, why are you still here? The kids should have been in bed an hour ago. We all have a big day tomorrow." When her husband didn't answer she moved closer waving her hand in front of him. "Michael?"

"He can't hear you." The bell-ringing Santa stepped behind her.

Melody screamed and dropped the cookie dough in the middle of the aisle, shattering the bowl. "Look what you made me do!"

"Easily fixed." Santa snapped his fingers and pieces of the bowl came back together. He waved his hand and the whole thing disappeared.

"Who are you?" Melody asked breathlessly.

"I am The Ghost of Christmas Present. I'm here to show you the gifts you're missing out on right now."

"Gifts? What gifts?" Melody thought of the pile of neatly wrapped packages she'd stacked in the attic away from prying eyes. None of them had come from a grocery store.

"Look." Santa pointed to Michael and Izzie. Izzie held up two bottles of decorative sprinkles. She looked like she was ready to cry again.

"What's wrong Izzie? It's a good idea. Mommy will be so happy if we help her make cookies for the party tomorrow."

Lizzie looked at the sprinkles in her hand. "I don't know if she wants the red and green sprinkles or the blue and silver ones."

"I'm sure either one would be fine. Or we could do some of both."

Izzie's pink cheeks sucked in as she tried to keep from crying. "I don't think Mommy wants me to make cookies with her. I can't do it right. I try my best, but I can't make them as pretty as she does."

"You make beautiful cookies."

"Mommy doesn't think so. She doesn't think anything I do is very good," Izzie said.

Melody covered her mouth. "Oh, baby."

Izzie looked down. "Besides, I already ruined Mommy's Christmas."

"Why would you say that?" Michael asked.

"Everything was all my fault. Grandma's cow broke, and the donkey, because I wasn't watching Devin, and then the toilet overflowed because I didn't watch Dallin, and then the dinner burned because she was trying to fix the mess I made."

Michael put his hand on her shoulder. "You didn't ruin Christmas, Iz. It's not your fault."

"Mommy said it was." A big tear rolled down Izzie's cheek.

Michael bent down and hugged her. "Mommy is just worried about the pageant."

Izzie shook her head hard against her father's shoulder. "I'm going to ruin the pageant too because I can't say my lines right. What if I mess up on stage? Mommy will be so mad. She wants everything to be perfect."

Michael pulled her against him. "Mommy loves you no matter what you do."

"Are you sure?" Izzie's eyes were magnified with tears.

He hugged her again. "Of course I'm sure."

Melody turned to the spirit. "Okay, so I messed up and I yelled at my kids. I was just trying to do my best. It doesn't mean I'm a bad mom, does it?"

Santa smiled at her. "I didn't say you were a bad mom or a good mom. I can only show you the things you need to see."

Melody looked down at her crying daughter with remorse. "It's been a stressful day. Everyone has bad days, right?"

"Funny you should mention bad days." The spirit waved his arm and the grocery store disappeared.

This time Melody was in a place that wasn't familiar. The building was old and dark and the walls were lined with blankets and sleeping figures. After a minute, Melody recognized it as the homeless shelter down the road from their church. From the mounds of sleeping people, a familiar face stood. Evelyn tiptoed to the door. A man was outside waiting for her.

"I didn't know Evelyn volunteered at the homeless shelter. No wonder she wanted us to help them," Melody said. "I feel bad that I had to tell her no. Inviting these people to our dinner and pageant would be a good thing. She should have said something earlier. If we'd had more time we could have—"

The spirit put his finger to his lips. "Listen."

Evelyn opened the door a crack and stepped outside. "It's freezing out here." She said to a man who was bundled up so tightly that Melody didn't recognize him. "You should come inside and get warm."

The man unzipped the front of his coat. It was Evelyn's husband, Tyler. "I can't. It's after hours. No men allowed."

"Do you have someplace warm to sleep tonight?" Evelyn asked.

"I'll be fine. As long as you and the kids are warm." Tyler blew on his fingers and leaned into the little heat spilling through the open door..

Evelyn indicated three sleeping figures on the floor. Melody recognized their three children, wrapped in quilts and lying on thing mats. "We're fine. Any luck today?"

He shook his head. "Everything is shutting down for Christmas. It'll probably be easier to find work after the holidays are over."

Evelyn nodded. "The Christmas pageant is tomorrow. At least we'll have a good meal and it's something for the kids to look forward to."

"It's probably the only Christmas they'll have this year." Tyler's voice was exhausted and he sounded defeated.

"We'll be fine. We have great people in our life, good friends, and each other." Evelyn glanced back over her shoulder at the full shelter. "Not everyone here is as blessed as we are."

Tyler leaned over and kissed her. "That's my girl. Counting her blessings even if it's only on one hand." He hugged her tight. "I'll see you tomorrow."

"Love you. Stay warm." Evelyn called after him. Her forehead wrinkled in worry as he stepped out into the cold and closed the door behind him.

"Why didn't she tell us? I would have—" Melody turned to the spirit, but he was gone. She was back in her warm house, in her nice kitchen. The bowl of cookie dough was sitting on the counter. She slumped into a kitchen chair and picked out a bit of cookie dough to eat, pondering everything she'd seen. Had she really been so busy that she was blind to other people's problems and her own blessings?

The grandfather clock chimed ten times.

7

Christmas Future

Melody stood and put the dough back in the fridge. It was too late and she was too overwhelmed by everything to start the cookies tonight. She'd have to wake up early and get them done. She turned off the light in the kitchen and walked into the living room.

The room had changed again. She was in a smaller living room with shabby carpet and old furniture. A pile of laundry lay on a worn leather couch. A little girl sat on the floor watching T.V.

"Oh, hi, Mom."

Melody turned as a young woman walked in cradling a phone and carrying a half-dressed toddler on her hip. For a second she thought it was another younger version of herself, but she'd never lived in a house like this.

"I don't have time to talk. I need to get Kate to school." The young woman shifted the baby to the other hip, prodded the child on the floor with her toe, and hissed, "You need to get ready." She leaned into the phone. "Christmas? No. I'm not going to be able to get the time off."

"Izzie?" Melody asked, suddenly understanding that she was looking at a grown version of her daughter. She stepped toward the young woman, but like the others, Grown-up Izzie couldn't hear her.

Izzie listened for a minute. "I'm sorry Mom. I know Dallin is out of the country and Devin's can't travel with his new baby, but we just can't do it this year." She continued to hold the phone to her ear, but it was clear she wasn't listening as the little girl tugged at her clothes.

"I'm hungry, Mama," the little girl said.

Izzy shook her head at the little girl. "Find your shoes. Daddy's making you a sandwich to eat on the way. Oh, not you mom. Yeah it's Kate. No, sorry, she doesn't have time to talk right now. She has to find her shoes." With the last words Izzie gestures to her daughter to hurry. "Yeah, I know, Mom. I try to make sure she puts everything back in the same place. Hooks and cubbies with the kids' names? We just don't have room for...right, good idea. Look, sorry, I need to get going...I know Mom. I miss you too. It's just not going to happen this year. I've got to go. I'll talk to you later. Love you." Grown-up Izzie sighed as she hung up the phone.

"Hey, was that your mom?" A young man who appeared to be Izzy's husband walked into the room. He handed the little girl a sandwich, kissed Izzy on the cheek, and took the baby from her.

"Yeah," Izzie knelt and dug through the pile of clothes on the couch.

"And you told her we couldn't come this year?" The young man said.

"Yep. Oh, finally." She held up a pair of red and green plaid shoes triumphantly.

Her husband balanced the baby in his arms. "Hey, I have an idea. Maybe your parents could come spend Christmas here. We could move Nichole's crib into our room for a few nights and Kate could sleep on the floor."

"No. Oh no," Izzie looked horrified at the thought.

"Why not?" he asked. "I think it might be fun for your parents to see the kids in their natural habitat for a change."

"Absolutely not!" Izzie stood up. "Do you have any idea what Christmas was like at my house when I was growing up?"

"No," her husband said, "tell me."

"In a word, it was perfect." Izzy said.

"That sounds terrible," her husband pushed the pile of clothes out of the way and sat down on the couch.

Izzie knelt on the floor to help her daughter into her shoes. "It really wasn't, but I can't imagine trying to do Christmas with my mom here. She's not going to understand that my house is a mess or the carpet is stained or that I had to order a pre-cooked Christmas dinner because I have to work overtime through the holidays. She'll see the mismatched ornaments and the plastic wreath and the one chintzy string of lights over the front porch and she'll know that her daughter is a complete and utter failure at Christmas." She slumped back against the couch.

He reached to rub her shoulders, but Izzy pulled away. "It's been a hard year and I really just need to relax over Christmas." She shook her head as she dug through the pile of clothes again. "My mom doesn't know the meaning of the word 'relax'."

Melody moved close to her daughter. "I'll understand, baby. I promise. The important thing is that we're together at Christmas."

Izzy pulled a satiny white coat from the pile of clothes and held it against her chest. It reminded Melody of Izzy's angel costume for the pageant. "I'll just never measure up to her level of perfection."

The word 'perfection' echoed through the small room.

8

Set Free

M elody opened her eyes. She was in her bed, fully clothed. She couldn't remember how she'd gotten there. Michael was asleep next to her. He must have carried her up to bed after she fell asleep on the couch. She sat up. The rattle of chains stopped her. She looked around for her mother, but couldn't see her.

Then she lifted her arms. Heavy, cold metal encircled her wrists.. She stared down in horror and disbelief. More chains crossed her chest. She moved the blanket and realized that lengths of chain covered her from her neck to her ankles. She tried to pry them off, but they wouldn't budge. Tears pricked at her eyes. She'd failed again. Her mother had warned her, but she hadn't learned what she was supposed to have learned last night. She lowered her chin to her chest. Her heart felt as heavy as the chains wrapped around her. She couldn't deny that she deserved every single link.

Despite the weight of the chains, she tried not to make too much noise as she got out of the bed. She stood in front of the bedroom window, staring at her reflection and the chains that encircled her arms and neck and waist. Her image faded into a hooded figure standing on the balcony. The figure beckoned for her to come out. Trembling, Melody opened the door and stepped into the cold night, dragging her chains behind her.

"You must be the ghost of Christmas Future, here to show me how I die unloved and unwanted, because I was selfishly trying to make Christmas perfect for myself instead of making it meaningful for my family."

The spirit slid its hood down. It was Melody's mom again. "No darling, nothing like that. But if you want to get rid of those chains, there is someone else we need to visit."

"Another ghost?" Melody asked.

"No, not a ghost, the only one who can break the chains that bind you, the Master of Christmas Past, Present and Future."

"What does that even mean?" Melody asked, but her mother was gone. Melody was standing on a long dirt road with a group of strangers dressed in worn earth-colored robes.

A ragged young man ran toward the group. "He's here, he's here." He gripped the shoulders of an old man. "I have seen him." He beckoned to the whole group. "Come! Come and see!"

The group of people looked at each other, murmuring words of disbelief. Some stayed behind. Others choose to follow the young man. Curious, Melody went with the group that followed. They walked for a long time on the dark road. Melody walked slowly, a few paces behind the group. She was tired, her chains were heavy, and they rattled and clanked with every step she took. She thought about turning back, but she didn't know where else to go. She followed the young man to the outskirts of an ancient town.

He stopped at a cave. There was a line of people waiting to look inside. One by one each of them stopped at the entrance to the cave. One by one, each of them fell to their knees. Melody was so far back that she couldn't see what caused them to react that way. Finally she got close enough to see past the crowd and into the cave. A young mother was sitting on the bare floor with a baby in her arms. A weary but proud man stood watch at their side.

Melody realized the people in front of her were placing gifts in front of the child; a few coins, a loaf of bread, a bit of cloth. The gifts weren't much, but Melody understood they were giving all they had. She searched her pockets, but found nothing to give. All she had were the chains wrapped around her body, weighing her down. She had no gift and the noise from her chains was disrupting the peace around her. She turned to leave, but the crowd pressed against her and she couldn't go.

Then was in front of the cave. She dropped to her knees, her face down, ashamed. "I'm sorry. I don't have a gift. I'm usually really good at finding the perfect thing for everyone, but now..." She stopped realizing how inadequate her apology was. She whispered, "I have nothing to give."

She closed her eyes against the tears as the scene before her changed again. She was in the twins' room, rocking a very small and very sick Dallin. She thought of all the sleepless nights she'd stayed up worrying over her kids. In another moment she was at church, teaching Bible stories to a squirrely bunch of three-year-olds who didn't seem to be listening. Next she was collecting cans for a food drive, then opening the door for a stranger, then bringing food to a sick friend. Finally she saw herself with Erin, tenderly caring for their mom in the last months of her life. As the sadness nearly overwhelmed her the scene shifted again. She saw herself in her own home, dancing around the kitchen with Michael and her kids and finding joy in just being together.

Her family's laughter faded into a reverent stillness as she watched herself kneel to place a basket of flowers on the headstone at her mother's grave. Above her mother's name was carved the scripture "Inasmuch as ye have done it unto the least of these, my brethren, ye have done it unto me."

Melody remembered when she and Erin had chosen that epitaph for her mother's grave. If anyone had embodied giving to the 'least of these' it was their mother. They'd never had much, but their mom was always helping someone with just a little bit less and many who had a lot more. She didn't care who she served. She gave her best to everyone around her.

Melody considered what the scripture meant in her own life. "Maybe I've done a few good things. But it's not enough. It will never be enough." Melody looked around her. She was no longer in the cemetery, but on the top of a hill. The baby was now a grown man in a white robe. He held His hands out to her so she could see the nail prints in His palms.

She couldn't look into His eyes. "I've made so many mistakes. I've hurt my family and neglected my friends and the people who needed me most. I tried to make Christmas perfect, but instead I made it meaningless." She kept her eyes on the ground. Her tears slid down her cheeks and fell on the wounds in His feet. "I don't have anything worth giving to you."

She felt His hand on her shoulder and she looked up. He gestured to the chains that lay across her shoulders. She looked at Him, confused. He gestured again.

"You want me to give you these? They aren't gifts, they're mistakes." Melody touched the chains, remembering what her mom had said, "Mistakes and regrets." Her soul felt as heavy as the chains that encircled her body. "They are so heavy and so hard to bear." The man continued to smile at her, waiting. She bowed her head again. "If you really want them, I guess I can let you take them."

She waited, but the chains weren't taken from her shoulders. She had somehow known they were too much for even Him to take away. Finally she looked up again. He was still waiting, watching her with a gentle smile.

He held out His hands again.

Suddenly she understood. "You can't take them from me, can you? I have to be willing to give them up."

He nodded.

Melody gripped the chains with trembling hands, but as she tried to remove them, she saw herself yelling at her children, arguing with her husband, and getting so swept up making the pageant perfect that she ignored Evelyn's obvious need. Her hands dropped to her side. "I can't make you take these. I was the one who made all the mistakes. I forged them myself."

"You don't have to carry them anymore." Her mother was back at Melody's side. This time her mother wore a long white robe. She no longer bore the chains that had encircled her earlier. "You can let them go. He's already paid for them. It's time to give them up."

Melody bowed her head and lifted the chains from her neck. Kind hands reached out to receive them. As soon as He touched the chains, the weight of her guilt and her inadequacy fell away. Love and gratitude for her Savior overwhelmed her. Her tears of sorrow were swept away in the magnitude of His love and grace.

She lifted her face to look at Him. "What happens when I make new chains?"

He placed His hand on Melody's cheek. "I will always be here to receive them. You just need to ask." Melody covered His hand with hers, feeling the prints of the nails in His palms.

9

Christmas Cookies

Melody moved her hand from her cheek. She felt the dampness against her pillow. She opened her eyes. The radiant light from her vision was replaced by the morning sun through her bedroom window. The bed next to her was empty. The house smelled like freshly baked cookies.

"The pageant!" She stood up and hurried to the stairs. She stopped at the top of the stairs and watched her family. The entire kitchen was covered in flour and cut out sugar cookies. Michael was pulling another batch out of the oven. Izzie was in the formal dining room. The elegant Christmas tablescape Melody had designed had been shoved aside to make room for a cookie decorating station. The twins were playing on the floor in piles of spilled flour. Melody was sure no one had had anything for breakfast but cookie dough. Everything was a complete and utter disaster and an absolute beauty to behold.

"Oh, you guys!" Melody exclaimed.

Everyone froze in place. For a moment Melody thought it was all part of another vision. "Can any of you hear me?"

After a couple of moments of silence Izzie answered, "Yeah, we can hear you Mommy."

Her gaze fell on each of them, one by one. The fear she saw in their eyes pierced her heart. She put on her biggest smile, started down the stairs and said, "What an awesome surprise! I was so worried about getting the cookies done, and here you all are. You let me sleep in and you started the cookies without me."

Michael looked at her guiltily. "I'm sorry about the mess, hon."

"It doesn't matter." Melody leaned over and gave him a big hug and a kiss, flour-covered apron and all.

She patted the two boys on the head and then walked over to examine Izzie's work. Izzie sat up straight, her big blue eyes full of worry. Some of the cookies were blobby, some had been over-decorated and there was definitely one or two that would make an interesting, "guess what this is supposed to be?" game at the party tonight. Melody bit off whatever threatened to come out of her mouth and said. "Oh, Izzie, these are beautiful!"

Izzie stayed frozen for a few beats, like she didn't understand the praise. Finally she said, "They aren't as good as the ones you make."

Melody picked one up and took a big bite. "They're better, because you made them with love. Love is the best ingredient you can put in cookies."

Izzie laughed with relief. "Thanks."

Melody turned away, still eating the cookie. She realized they did taste better than the ones she'd made before, even if they were over-frosted or lop-sided. "I'm going to get dressed and then I want to help."

She looked at the clock and remembered what she'd seen the night before. "But I need to make a couple of quick phone calls first."

10

Imperfect Perfection

"This is Melody, our miracle worker." Kara gushed to the well-dressed woman who stood next to her. "She did all of this." She spread her arms to encompass the whole scene. "Melody, this is my mom visiting for Christmas. I've been telling her about all of the amazing things that you do."

"This is certainly the epitome of holiday cheer. Everything is so beautiful," the woman said.

"It's a bit over-the-top." Melody replied. She was suddenly embarrassed by all the excess.

"It is perfectly beautiful, and obviously created with love," the older woman said smiling. She put her hand on Melody's arm. "And it's okay to take the compliment."

Melody smiled back. "Thank you. It was a lot of work, but it was also a lot of fun to put together. I hope everyone enjoys it."

"And these must be your homemade cookies," Kara pointed at the plastic bin in Melody's hands. "I heard Jenna flaked on us at the last minute. It doesn't matter, your cookies have always been better than hers anyway."

"Actually Jenna's family is sick." Melody moved to the desert table where tiered gold serving trays waited to receive the cookies. She hesitated for a second while Kara and her mother watched. She thought about the cookies she was carrying. All had been made with love, but all were glaringly imperfect.

From across the room she caught Izzie watching her. Melody smiled at her daughter and then opened the bin with a flourish. "And I didn't make the cookies, or at least not all of them. My whole family helped. I couldn't have done it without them." Izzie returned her smile and then disappeared into the dressing room.

Melody tried not to let the look of dismay on Kara's face get to her.

"They're quite unique." Kara's mom picked up a cookie and turned it from side to side, like she was trying to decipher what it was. "Kara used to love making cookies with me when she was a little girl."

"I did," Kara said it like she'd just remembered. "It was my favorite part of Christmas. But I wasn't very good at it."

"You were great at it. Of course, cookie making with kids is always quite a mess." Kara's mother said.

"Yes, it is." Melody thought of the piles of unwashed dishes and flour-covered floors and countertops she'd left at home.

"But it's worth every bit of spilled flour and every sticky fingerprint. Your little ones grow up so fast, trust me." Kara's mother squeezed her daughter's arm.

"We'd better find a place to sit." Kara says. "You won't believe the costumes Melody put together, she hand painted all of the sets, and..."

As they walked away, Melody considered everything—the food, the decorations, the sets, and the costumes. She shook her head as she remembered how much time she put into it and how much pressure and stress she put on herself to make it perfect. She looked around the room, knowing there were talented people who could have helped, people she assumed were too busy or too unskilled to create what she had envisioned.

Next year.

That thought brought her back to the other person she needed to talk to. Evelyn was near the stage, coaxing her son into a sheep costume.

"Evelyn," Melody said, her smile wide and genuine. "I wanted to apologize for not listening to you yesterday. I think sharing our pageant and our meal with—"

A disruption at the door stopped her from finishing that sentence. Amy was arguing with an older woman dressed in a faded blue dress. The woman stood just inside the door. "But we were invited," she insisted.

"I don't think—" Amy looked to Melody for help..

"Hello, Mrs. Hansen," Melody said, coming to the door. "I'm so glad to see you made it."

The woman looked a little surprised that Melody knew her name. "Oh, yes. Of course. I'm here."

"Can I help you find a seat?" Melody took the woman's arm.

Amy stood dumbfounded, Another woman came in. Then young woman with two small children. Then a man with a scruffy beard and a shabby overcoat. They came in slowly, eyes warry, like they were afraid someone was going to throw them out. "Melody, I thought we agreed—"

"We were wrong," Melody said.

"But what about the food?" Amy looked over the growing crowd. "There won't possibly be enough for everyone."

"We have plenty and if not, Michael's picking up a bunch of pizzas. I think the kids would prefer that anyway."

"I can't believe you would—" Amy began, but Melody shushed her as the children's choir began their warm up song.

More people filled in the back. Michael came in, his arms loaded with pizzas. Melody directed him to the kitchen just before the pageant began. They found a place in the back of the room as the lights dimmed.

Michael put his arm around Melody. "I'm so glad I could be here for this."

She leaned her head against his shoulder. "Me too."

Melody sat back to watch the pageant. She looked at the full chairs, at the people she knew and the people she hoped she could get to know better. The lights came up and the children moved onto the stage, portraying Mary and Joseph. Melody was caught up in the story as she never had been. The shepherds assembled and a white-robed Izzie glided onto the stage. Melody held her breath.

Izzie hesitated and then delivered the line. "For us a child is born."

Melody's heart sank in disappointment. Then she saw the panic on Izzie's face and gave her a quick thumbs up. She reconsidered the line. "Unto us a Child is born" was from the scriptures, but "for us a Child is born' almost conveyed a different meaning.

"She's right." Melody said to Michael. "He really was born for us, to take away all our sins and sorrows, our regrets and really, all of our failings. He came to make us better than we could ever be alone."

Michael leaned over and kissed her cheek, "Yes, He did."

Melody looked up and saw her mom with her arm around Izzie. Above the sweet voices of the children's choir Melody could hear her mother's voice: joining in:

My chains are gone, I've been set free

My God, my Savior has ransomed me

And like a flood His mercy reigns

Unending love

Amazing grace[1]

       Louie Giglio and Chris Tomlin

~The End~

About the Author

Jennifer Shaw Wolf grew up in the tiny town of Wilford, Idaho where she spent many cold dark winter mornings milking cows and many cozy evenings by the fire reading anything she could get her hands on. (Once the cows were milked of course). She graduated from Ricks College in Rexburg, Idaho and Brigham Young University in Provo, Utah with a degree in communications. She's mom to four now grown kids, three kids-in-law, a beautiful granddaughter and one spoiled dog. She lives with the love of her life and husband of 30+ years in the beautiful forests of Western Washington. Her dearest loves are her family, her books, and her faith. She's the author of three young adult mysteries and the Emerson Fox Cozy Mystery Series. "Mom's Christmas Carol" is her first inspirational novella.

To read more of her books, join her newsletter, or just chat, check out jennifershawwolf.com.